Weekly Reader Children's Book Club presents

IS MILTON MISSING?

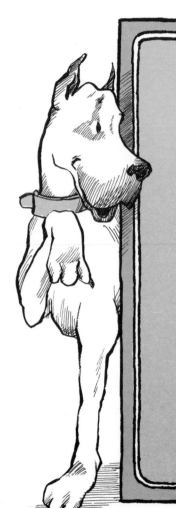

IS MILTON

Text copyright © 1975 by Steven Kroll
Illustrations copyright © 1975 by Dick Gackenbach
All rights reserved
Printed in the United States of America

*Library of Congress
Cataloging in Publication Data*

Kroll, Steven.
Is Milton missing?
SUMMARY: Richard searches all over the apartment for
his dog but Milton is nowhere to be found. Then he tries
the apartment next door.
[1. Dogs—Fiction]   I. Gackenbach, Dick, ill.
II. Title.
PZ7.K9225Is   [E]   75-4586
ISBN 0-8234-0261-4

Weekly Reader Children's Book Club Edition

MISSING?

STORY BY STEVEN KROLL
PICTURES BY DICK GACKENBACH

HOLIDAY HOUSE · NEW YORK

For Margery, who made it possible

When Richard got home from school, his
Great Dane wasn't there. "Oh no," thought
Richard. "Where could Milton be?"

Richard sat down in a chair by the door.
Milton had been his dog for a whole year.
He'd come to live with Richard as a puppy.

Together Richard and Milton had gone
for long walks in the park.

As Milton grew older, Daisy would come too.
Daisy was Mrs. Foster's Great Dane.

All three had played on the floor in Richard's room.

Sometimes Richard and Milton and Daisy
had followed other people down the street.

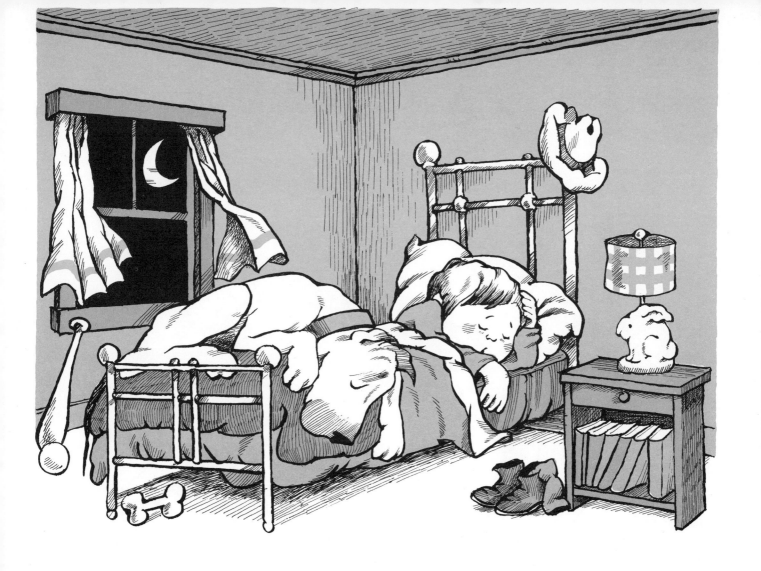

At night, Milton slept on a special blanket
at the foot of Richard's bed.

Every day, when Richard came home from school, Milton would meet him at the door.

But where was Milton now? Richard went to his room. Everything seemed to be in place. But the window was wide open. Could Milton have jumped out?

Richard rushed to the window. He looked down
three stories. There were no people. There was
no Milton. There was just sidewalk.
No, Milton had not jumped out.

Could Milton be in the bathroom?

Richard dashed in and peeked behind the shower curtain. No, Milton was not in the bathroom.

Maybe he was in the hall closet.

Richard opened the door. A whole pile of stuff
slid out at his feet. Richard pushed it all back in.
He could barely get the door closed. But still
there was no Milton.

Richard looked in the living room.
Could Milton be under the rug?

No, he wasn't under the rug or behind the
sofa. There was just a lot of dust.

Maybe he was in the bedroom where
Richard's parents slept.

Richard looked under the bed, but
all he could find was an old bone.

Could Milton be in the kitchen?

Richard looked in the kitchen.
The dish beside the table was empty.
But, no Milton.

Richard wondered what to do now.

Then he had a thought. Maybe Daisy
was missing too.

He ran across the hall to Mrs. Foster's.
He rang the bell. No answer.
He turned the knob. The door opened!

Richard stepped inside. No one was there.
Was Mrs. Foster missing too?
Then he heard noises.
They seemed to come from the kitchen.

He crept down the hall.
The noises got louder. And louder. AND LOUDER.
Richard pushed open the kitchen door.
And there . . .

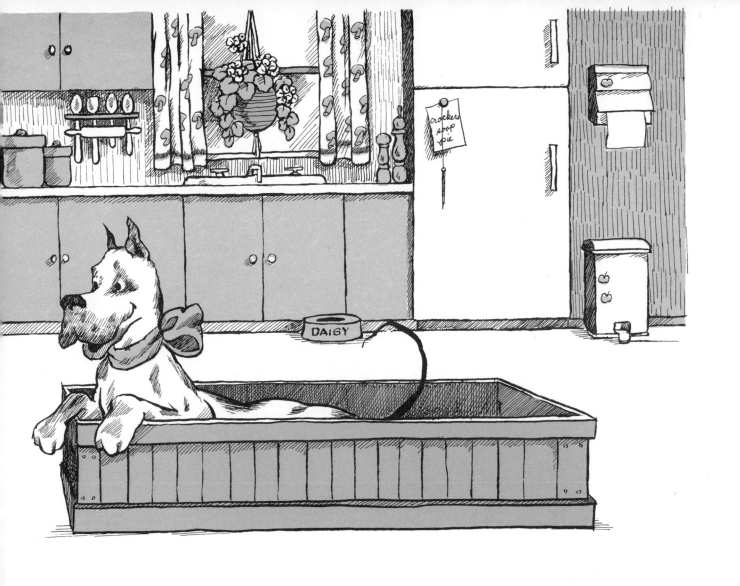

was everybody. Milton. Mrs. Foster. Daisy.

And five little Great Dane puppies!